Teelo's Adventures

A Cat Adrift

Story by Maria Coffey
Art by Eugenie Fernandes

Annick Press Ltd.
Toronto • New York • Vancouver

We acknowledge the support of the Canada Council for the Arts, the Ontario Arts Council, and the Government of Canada through the Book Publishing Industry Development Program (BPIDP) for our publishing activities.

Cataloging in Publication Data

Coffey, Maria, 1952-
A cat adrift

(Teelo's adventures)
ISBN 1-55037-727-2 (bound).--ISBN 1-55037-726-4 (pbk.)

I. Fernandes, Eugenie, 1943- II. Title. III. Series: Coffey, Maria, 1952- .
Teelo's adventures.

PS8555.O2873C267 2002   jC813'.54   C2001-903529-2
PZ7.C6585Caa 2002

The art in this book was rendered in watercolor.
The text was typeset in Seagull.

Distributed in Canada by:
Firefly Books Ltd.
3680 Victoria Park Avenue
Willowdale, ON
M2H 3K1

Published in the U.S.A. by:
Annick Press (U.S.) Ltd.
Distributed in the U.S.A. by:
Firefly Books (U.S.) Inc.
P.O. Box 1338, Ellicott Station
Buffalo, NY 14205

Printed and bound in Canada by
Friesens, Altona, Manitoba.

visit us at: **www.annickpress.com**

For Allen and his great-granddaughter Lilian,
with fond memories of sunny days in Ballet Bay.
—M.C.

For my old sailing buddies Charlie, Billy,
Donnie, and Gail.
—E.F.

It was breakfast time on Cloud Island. Victor the Vet hurried about, feeding all the animals who lived with him in his snug little house. As he ran out of the door, he scooped up the cat and gave him a hug.

"Look after the house while I'm away, Teelo," he said.

Teelo watched Victor paddle off to the city in his kayak. Then he went back inside for his breakfast. And there, perched on his bowl, was ...

A RAT! Teelo sprang at the rat, but it scurried out of reach. Snarling and spitting, he chased it all over the house – past Ruby the Rooster and Sylvie the Snake, through the hens' eggs, across Terry the Terrier's basket, around and around Bonaparte the Parrot, and right out of the door.

He chased the rat up a tree, to the tip of a long skinny branch. When Teelo was about to pounce on the rat ...

Ccccc-rrrack! The branch snapped, and Teelo and the rat tumbled into the sea.

Big waves washed over Teelo's head; he flailed and spluttered, and he almost sank. Luckily, a log came floating by, and Teelo scrambled onto it. But when he shook the water from his eyes, he realized that he was still in trouble. The log was drifting away from Cloud Island, taking Teelo with it.

Cloud Island grew smaller and smaller, until finally it disappeared. The sun sank below the horizon, turning the sea to gold. Teelo was lost in a wilderness of water where unfamiliar creatures lived. Furry, bright-eyed sea otters swam on their

backs, cradling their babies. Puffins with bulbous orange beaks whirred past like windup toys. And gigantic gray whales cruised by, their breath spouting high into the air.

Night fell, and a sliver of moon appeared beneath a great glistening blanket of stars. Teelo was cold and hungry, and very lonely.

He closed his eyes, and was dreaming about his snug little house when BOOM! Thunder crashed around Teelo's ears and bright lightning fizzed across the sky. Wind whipped the sea into whitecapped waves and rain lashed down, soaking Teelo in seconds. Terrified, he clung with all his might to the wildly tossing log.

At last the storm blew over, and the gray light of
dawn seeped into the sky. Teelo slumped on the log,
filled with despair. Suddenly, he heard a strange sound.

CREAK. He looked up, but there was nothing ahead save sea and sky. CR-EAK! He looked around ...

... and gliding along behind him, rocking gently on the swell, was a wooden boat. It had sails like huge bat wings, a carved dragon on its bow, and smoke curling from its stovepipe. On deck were a little girl with wide brown eyes and an old man with flowing white hair.

"Well, I'll be darned, Lilly," said the man. "Here's a cat adrift. Those pesky creatures get everywhere!"

Lilly climbed down a ladder and lifted Teelo from the log. She carried him below decks to the cabin, where she dried him by the stove.

"Cats are a nuisance," grumbled the old man. "They make me sneeze. ACHOO!"

"But Grandpa!" pleaded Lilly. "He's got nowhere else to go."

Grandpa blew his nose loudly.

"All right, he can stay. But *only* until the end of summer. When we get back to the city dock, you'll have to get rid of him."

For weeks they sailed across a sea as flat as silk. Teelo was happy on the boat. Lilly caught fish for him and fed him the last of Grandpa's cream. They played hide-and-seek, and Teelo spent hours swatting at seagulls flying by.

But when Teelo scrambled up the mast and got tangled in the rigging, Grandpa was furious.

"Pesky cat!" he cried. "We should have left him on that log!"

That evening, though, when Teelo curled up with Lilly on her bunk, Grandpa took out his ukulele and sang them both to sleep with songs about the sea.

One morning Grandpa turned the boat around.

"Summer's nearly over," he told Lilly. "Soon we'll be living at the city dock again, and you'll be back at school. But as for this cat – *ACHOO!*"

Lilly held Teelo tightly, and stared out to sea.

They sailed on until the city appeared in the distance. As they passed a tiny island, Teelo saw a snug little house with windows that winked in the sunlight. He looked again and saw a dog digging in the sand, hens and a rooster scratching through the seaweed, a snake stretched over a rock, a parrot perched on a branch, and a man kayaking to shore. It was Cloud Island!

To get an even better look, Teelo ran right to the tip of the bowsprit. At that moment the boat lurched against a wave, and Teelo tumbled into the water.

Waves washed over Teelo's head; he flailed and spluttered, and he almost sank. Luckily, Victor came by in his kayak, scooped up Teelo, and paddled him to the beach.

There, crowding around him, were his old friends: Sylvie the Snake, Terry the Terrier, Bonaparte the Parrot, Ruby the Rooster, and the hens. They were so excited, at first they didn't notice the little girl with wide brown eyes and the old man with flowing white hair rowing up behind them. Until ...

ACHOO! They all turned around, and Teelo dashed across the sand and into Lilly's arms.

"Thank you for saving my cat!" Lilly cried.

"*Your* cat?" said Victor. "But Teelo is *my* cat. He's been lost for weeks. I've looked everywhere for him."

Grandpa explained about finding Teelo adrift on a log. Victor thanked him and Lilly for bringing Teelo home. Lilly said nothing. She bent her head, and hid her tears in Teelo's long, wet fur.

"Oh dear," said Victor. "Please don't cry. I can see you love Teelo, and that he loves you, too."

Lilly nodded.

"I'm terribly fond of Teelo," Victor went on, "but ... well ... if you promise to visit us often ... maybe ..." Victor swallowed hard. "Maybe you should keep Teelo."

Lilly looked up.

"I can't keep him," she whispered. "Grandpa doesn't like cats. They make him sneeze."

Grandpa blew his nose loudly.

"That's true," he agreed. "But as cats go, this one isn't so bad. I suppose he's worth a few sneezes. *ACHOO!*"

So Teelo became a live-aboard cat. On weekends he often sailed over to Cloud Island to visit his friends, and in the summers they all went sailing together. Victor took the tiller, Terry the Terrier barked at birds, Sylvie the Snake curled around the bowsprit, Ruby the Rooster and the hens cuddled on the cabin top, Bonaparte the Parrot commandeered the crow's nest, Teelo and Lilly watched out for floating logs ...

and Grandpa's sneezes could be heard for miles around.